MW00489839

Who Will Help?

by Helen Young
illustrated by Craig Smith

SCHOOL PUBLISHERS

Printed in China

ISBN 10: 0-15-350610-5
ISBN 13: 978-0-15-350610-9

Ordering Options
ISBN 10: 0-15-350598-2 (Grade 1 On-Level Collection)
ISBN 13: 978-0-15-350598-0 (Grade 1 On-Level Collection)
ISBN 10: 0-15-357754-1 (package of 5)
ISBN 13: 978-0-15-357754-3 (package of 5)

4 5 6 7 8 9 10   0940   15 14 13 12 11 10 09

One day, Fox said,
"Here is a ball, Cat."

"Here is a jet, Dog.
Here is a doll, Pig."

They had a good time.
Mom called out,
"Let's eat!"

"Who will help me
pick up?" asked Fox.
Cat was first to go
home.

Then Pig went home,
too.
"I will help," said Dog.

"Dog, you helped,"
said Mom.
"Will you eat here?"

"Thank you!" said Dog.
"I like eating here!"